This book belongs to

....

make believe ideas ltd

The Wilderness, Berkhamsted, Hertfordshire, HP4 2AZ, UK.
6th Floor, South Bank House, Barrow Street, Dublin 4, D04 TR29, Ireland.

www.makebelieveideas.co.uk

Written by Rosie Greening.
Illustrated by Lara Ede.

SANTA CLAWS

Lara Ede • Rosie Greening

make
believe
ideas

In the land of the **growlers**
and **clawers** and **roarers**,
lived **REX**, the **friendliest**

TYRANNOSAURUS.

Tricera Hilltops

Carnotaurus Close

Dippy Lake

N
W   E
S

He really loved CHRISTMAS
(as all dinos do) –
the eating and munching
and lunch-crunching too.

Paleozoic Ruins

Raptor Forest

Mount Vesaurus

Dino Land

The dinosaurs **thought** they had **CHRISTMASTIME** covered.
But there were some **things** that they **hadn't discovered.**

NO stockings.
NO wrapping.
NO Christmassy List.

In **DINO LAND**,
presents
just didn't
EXIST!

So, REX thought that Christmas
was sometimes quite BORING.
The DINOS just ate
'til they ended up snoring!

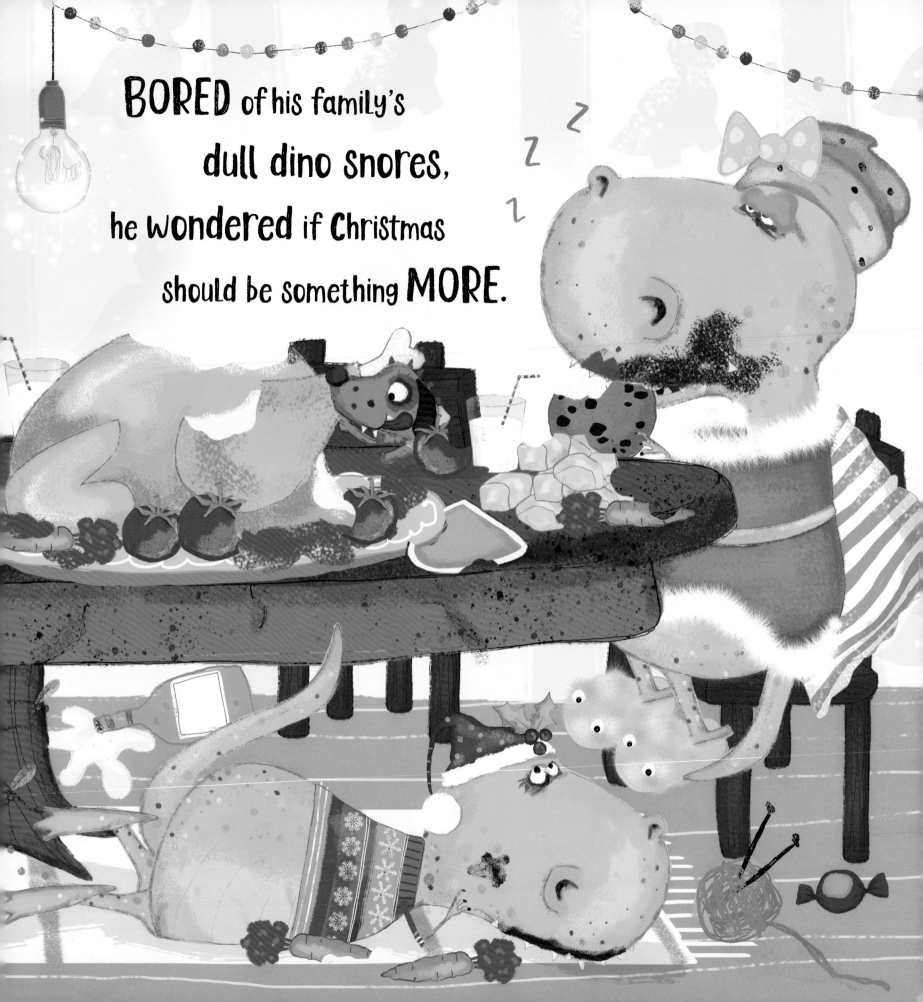

BORED of his family's dull dino snores, he wondered if Christmas should be something MORE.

So, **SOCK** after **SOCK**, his toes nice and warm,

REX went for a stroll
in the **cold, snowy storm.**

Soon, he passed **STEG** at her trendy toy store.
She told him, "I can't **feel my feet** anymore!"

Steg's Toys

REX loved to help,
so he said,
"Please take these!
I've got LOTS of socks
and don't want you to
FREEZE."

Then REX passed RAPTOR who baked gingerbread.
"I can't ice these shapes when I'm COLD!" RAPTOR said.

Gingerbread

REX said, "Don't worry, try THESE socks for size." RAPTOR was thrilled with the cosy SURPRISE.

REX soon passed DIPPY
and his **gem** collection.
He needed a **bag**
for his **newest** selection.

REX said to DIPPY,
"I've got an idea."

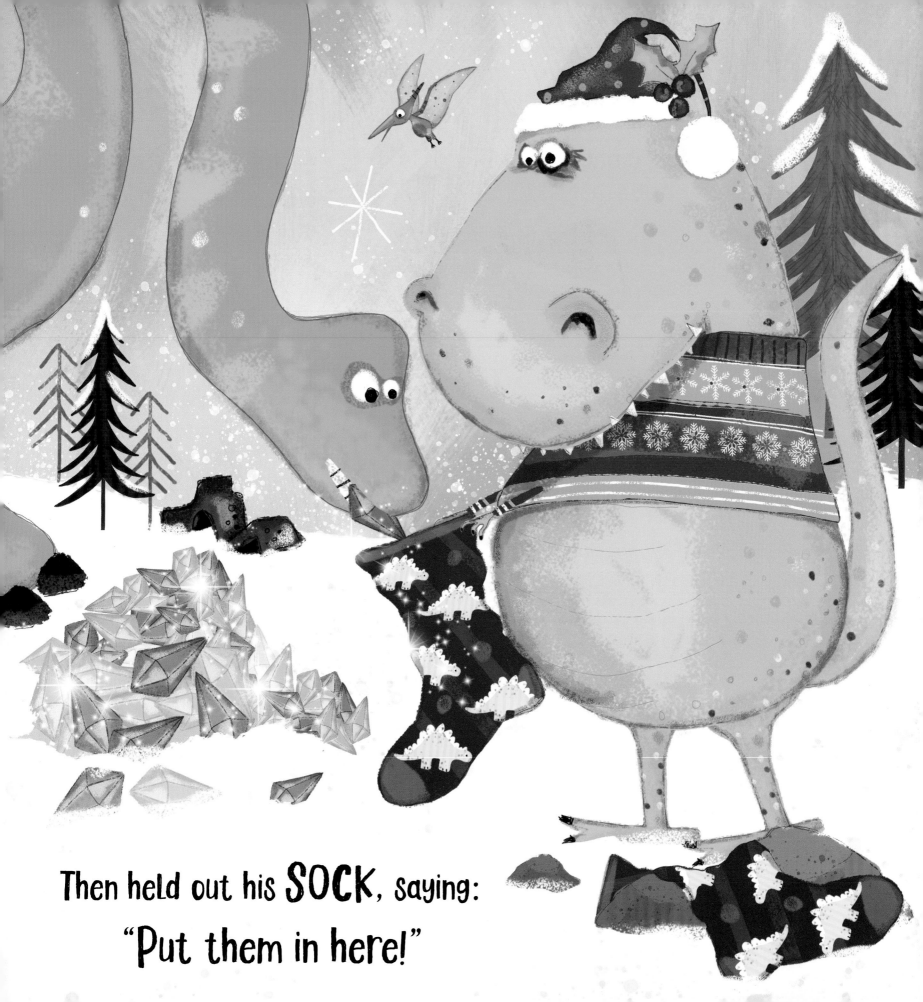

Then held out his **SOCK**, saying:
"Put them in here!"

The sun started sinking, so REX turned to go.
His feet were like ICE as he trudged through the snow.

But, when REX got home, he was in for a SHOCK...

His friends had returned

ALL his SNUGGLY SOCKS.

And tucked in each SOCK
was a thank-you gift too.

It filled **REX** with joy:
now **he knew what to do!**

REX found more socks (he had PLENTY to spare).
He SECRETLY stuffed them and hung them with care.

The very next morning,
when **Christmas Day** came,

the **DINOS** found gifts
in a **SOCK**
with their **name!**

From then on, the DINOS
hung SOCKS up each year,
which REX filled in secret
to spread JOY and cheer.

Paleozoic Ruins

Raptor Forest

Dino Land

But **REX** didn't want
any thanks or applause,

so he signed
all the presents:

*love
Santa Claws* x